SURVIVING LOVE! LIFE! DEATH!

A RELATIONSHIP REBOOT.

JOJO D'SOUZA

Dedication

To those who have loved deeply and made it work, and to those who have courageously parted ways - Whatever path you took, you have rebooted your lives, and that itself is a wonderful step forward.

Your journeys of love, resilience, and self-discovery inspire us all.

This book is for you.

- Jojo D'Souza

Contents

Foreword

"Surviving Love! Life! Death!" is a story about love, challenges, and the strength to start over. I'd like to take you on a journey with George and Radhika, two people from different backgrounds who fall in love against all odds.

This story digs deep into the heart of what it means to love and be loved, to face unimaginable trials, and to find the strength to rebuild when everything seems lost.

Amidst all our struggles, there is always hope. Hope that love can be rekindled, that wounds can heal, and that the journey, no matter how filled with obstacles, is always worth it.

This book shows the ups and downs of long-term relationships, the pain of separation, and the hard work it takes to heal and rebuild. It's honest about the tough times but also full of hope, reminding us that love is always worth fighting for.

Preface

From the sun-kissed shores of Goa, I have always found inspiration in the vibrant colours and moods of life and definitely of people.. The profound connections that bind us together. Storytelling has been a lifelong passion—a way to explore the depths of human emotion and the resilience of the human spirit.

In writing "Surviving Love! Life! Death!" I wanted to capture the essence of love in its many forms: the exhilarating highs, the heart-wrenching lows, and the often challenging journey of growth and redemption.

"This story is a reflection of many observations of love that I have witnessed, both enduring and lost, and the strength it takes to rebuild and start anew."

George and Radhika's story is not just a tale of romance but a tribute to the complexities of relationships. It is for everyone who has ever fought to make love work or had the courage to begin again. Through their journey, I hope to convey that love is a powerful force, capable of overcoming even the most daunting obstacles.

As you turn the pages, I invite you to reflect on your own experiences of love, life, and resilience. May this book inspire you to cherish the connections you hold dear and find the strength to face the challenges that come your way.

~ Jojo D'Souza, Author

Prologue

"Love can be a powerful force, uniting us in ways we never imagined."

For George Ferns and Radhika Rani Mehta, their love story began as a beautiful dream but soon faced the harsh realities of life. As they navigated through challenges and heartaches, their bond was tested like never before.

"It's a story about the resilience needed to mend what's broken or have the strength to start anew."

Join George and Radhika as they explore the true nature of love and the choices that shaped their lives.

CHAPTER ONE

An Unlikely Meeting

In the heart of Mumbai, where the vibrant pulse of the city never seemed to falter, lived a man whose passion for life was as boundless as the city itself. George Ferns, a football-loving techie, had always embraced the modern world with open arms. His Roman Catholic upbringing in the heart of the urban jungle had instilled in him a sense of freedom and adventure. Weekends found him on the football pitch, where his fierce competitiveness and love for the game were on full display - a stark contrast to the meticulous precision he brought to his work in the tech industry.

George was the epitome of modernity. His flat, a sleek blend of glass and steel, overlooked the sprawling cityscape. He thrived in the chaos, relishing every opportunity to explore new technologies, attend the latest sporting events, and immerse himself in the vibrant nightlife that Mumbai offered. To his friends, he was the life of every gathering, his infectious energy and easy charm drawing people to him like moths to a flame.

In another part of the city, where tradition held a firm grip on the rhythms of daily life, lived Radhika Rani Mehta. The daughter of a successful business family, Radhika's world was one of quiet elegance and disciplined simplicity. Her beauty was striking, but it was her brilliance and straightforward nature that truly set her apart. Shy and reserved, she navigated the conservative confines of her Hindu upbringing with grace and poise, her mind a wellspring of ideas that constantly sought expression.

Radhika's home was a sanctuary of tradition. The Mehta residence, with its intricately carved wooden doors and lush gardens, was a testament to her family's heritage. Inside, the aroma of incense mingled with the soft strains of classical music, creating an atmosphere of serene reverence. Radhika's days were filled with the responsibilities of managing her family's affairs, her sharp intellect and unwavering dedication earning her the respect of those around her.

Their worlds were as different as night and day, yet fate, with its strange sense of irony, had plans to bring them together.

Saturday, 10th July 2010, marked the opening of TechCon 2010, a prestigious technology conference held in the vibrant city of Mumbai. This annual event, renowned for showcasing cutting-edge innovations and fostering collaboration among tech enthusiasts, attracted the brightest minds from across the country. The theme for the year was "Innovating the Future," a nod to the rapid advancements in technology shaping the new decade.

The conference took place at the sprawling Mumbai Convention Centre, where attendees from diverse fields gathered to share insights, explore new ideas, and discuss the latest trends in technology. The atmosphere buzzed with excitement as innovators, industry leaders, and tech enthusiasts mingled, exchanging ideas and forging new connections.

Among the crowd was George Ferns, a passionate techie with a keen interest in blockchain and artificial intelligence.

George, known for his enthusiasm and expertise, was eager to immerse himself in the discussions and debates that would unfold over the weekend. As a Roman Catholic from a modern background, he was not only there to learn but also to network and potentially collaborate on future projects.

On the other side of the convention hall was Radhika Rani Mehta, a brilliant young woman with a keen mind and an equally sharp wit. She was the daughter of Mr Adil Bhai Hira Ram Mehta, a successful business man who had also co-sponsored the event. Radhika was no stranger to the world of innovation and entrepreneurship. Despite her conservative Hindu upbringing, she had always been fascinated by technology and its potential to transform society. Her father always took her along as Radhika was completing a Bachelors degree in Computer Science and Adil Bhai felt less of a technophobe when she was around.

Their paths first crossed during a panel discussion on "The Role of AI and Blockchain in Modern Business." George, eager to share his thoughts, engaged in a lively debate with the panelists, catching Radhika's attention. Intrigued by his insights and confidence, Radhika found herself drawn to the discussions.

George, ever the social butterfly, was in his element. He moved through the crowd with ease, engaging in animated discussions about the latest advancements in artificial intelligence and blockchain technology. His enthusiasm was palpable, his eyes lighting up with each new idea.

Radhika's reserved nature was definitely at odds with the chaotic energy of the event. As she moved through the crowds, she felt a mix of curiosity and nervousness, her sharp mind absorbing the wealth of information being presented through various sessions.

At one point, George found himself in a particularly lively discussion led by another tech enthusiast named David Kapoor. David, with his confident posture and loud voice, was holding court, impressing the group with his knowledge of blockchain and AI.

"And that's why blockchain is the future of secure transactions," David proclaimed, looking around to gauge the effect of his words.

It was then that he spotted Radhika, sitting quietly at the edge of the group, dressed in simple Indian attire that contrasted sharply with the modern, business-like garb of the other attendees. She seemed out of place, her shy demeanour making her an easy target for David's showmanship.

"Ah, we have a newcomer here!" David announced, his eyes gleaming with the prospect of further showing off. "Tell me, miss, what do you think about the introduction of blockchain and its impact on our financial systems?"

Radhika looked up, her eyes meeting David's with a mix of uncertainty and determination. She stood, her voice soft but clear. "Blockchain certainly has the potential to revolutionise secure transactions, but its real strength lies in decentralising trust and creating immutable records. However, it's not without its challenges, such as scalability and regulatory hurdles."

David was stumped, but recovered quickly, as everyone around gasped in awe. Sensing an opportunity to shine further, David hit back with a retort. "Oh, really? And how do you propose we overcome these so-called challenges? Surely you must have some innovative ideas, Ha Ha! You look timid, but you mean to say you understand what I'm talking about?."

Radhika didn't falter. She looked at him straight-faced and replied "For scalability, sharding techniques and off-chain solutions like the Lightning Network for Bitcoin are being explored. I guage that by the year 2015 there will be some white papers on this. As for regulatory issues, collaboration between technologists and policymakers is crucial to developing frameworks that balance innovation with security."

The room grew quiet as everyone listened intently. David, realising that Radhika's points were well-founded and beyond his depth, tried to regain control of the conversation. "But what about AI integration with blockchain? It's a complex intersection that even experts struggle with."

Radhika's eyes sparkled with confidence. "AI can enhance blockchain by providing advanced analytics for better decision-making and predictive capabilities. For instance, AI can help identify patterns and anomalies in transaction data, improving security and efficiency. The key is to develop algorithms that can work in tandem with decentralised networks without compromising their integrity."

A silence settled over the group as David struggled to come up with a counterpoint. He finally conceded, bowing slightly and clapping. "Well said, miss. It appears we have an expert among us." He excused himself and charged out of the room in a huff.

Radhika blushed, the attention making her self-conscious, but she held her ground, her poise and knowledge earning her the respect of the group.

George, watching from a distance, was captivated by the exchange. He admired Radhika's intelligence and the grace with which she handled herself. As the crowd applauded

Radhika and then began to disperse, he approached her, his smile warm and genuine.

"That was impressive," George said, extending his hand. "I'm George."

Radhika smiled back, shaking his hand. "Radhika Rani Mehta."

"Rani, like in Queen?" George said, beaming with curiosity.

Radhika looked at him with a frown, suppressing a half-smile that was forming on her face.

At that moment Radhika's father, entered.

Their meeting, sparked by this unexpected confrontation, ended there.

George, quickly understanding the situation, said, "Rani, give me your number."

"Maybe at the next Tech Conference in Goa, if you're going to be there," she replied and smiled as she turned and left to go home with her father.

CHAPTER TWO

A Cheesy Beginning

What seemed like forever was actually just around five months away. On Wednesday, December 15th, 2010, the Bogmalo Beach Heritage played host to #Null, a renowned tech conference attracting programmers, tech gurus, hackers, cybersecurity experts, AI pioneers, and blockchain enthusiasts from around the world. The atmosphere was electric, with animated conversations, the hum of high-tech demonstrations, and the click of keyboards filling the air.

Bogmalo Beach, close to Dabolim International Airport, offered the perfect setting. Its serene white sands, clear waters, and a few shacks serving local cuisine provided a tranquil backdrop. The Bogmalo Beach Heritage, with modern facilities, private parking, and easy road access, was right on the beach and boasted a fantastic view of the Arabian Sea. The resort's poolside area was renowned for its stunning sunsets.

In a bustling corner of the venue, Radhika was enjoying the ambience with her father by her side. Despite his conservative and protective nature, he was always immensely proud of his daughter. The resort's lounge area, with its warm lighting and relaxed vibe, provided a perfect backdrop for their presence.

George entered the lounge area about twenty minutes later. His eyes scanned the room, and his face lit up when he saw Radhika. Somehow, he liked Radhika. He liked her very much. As he began walking towards her table, his heartbeat quickened with each step.

Radhika glanced up just as George was closing the distance between them. Their eyes met briefly, and a small, welcoming smile appeared on her face. Just then, David cut in, bursting with energy and almost knocking over a waiter in his enthusiasm.

"Radhika Rani Mehta! India's most genius hidden talent,"

David shouted loudly, drawing the attention of nearby attendees. He was brilliant at opening lines, especially with parents, though he found mothers easier to charm. David's larger-than-life presence seemed to fill the entire lounge area as he approached the table.

David extended a hand towards Radhika's father with a beaming smile. "Mr Mehta, it's an honour to meet you! Your support as a co-sponsor for this event is invaluable. Thank you for believing in the power of technology and innovation," he gushed, his words flowing smoothly. He was piling on the praise like someone pouring on butter, thick and heavy, to flatter.

Radhika's father, though reserved, nodded politely. "Thank you, David. I don't always understand what all this technology is about, but I find it fascinating. That's why I always sponsor events like this and the previous conference in Mumbai as well," he replied, his voice steady with a hint of pride.

George, standing a few steps away, watched the interaction unfold with a mix of amusement and slight frustration. David had an uncanny knack for dominating any situation, and George knew it would be tough to get a word in. Radhika, noticing George, gave him a small wave. George took this as his cue and stepped forward, his heart pounding but his resolve firm. "Hello, Radhika," he said warmly, "It's good to see you again."

David, not one to miss an opportunity, turned to George with a wide grin. "Ah, George! Perfect timing. I was just about to discuss Radhika's brilliant insights on AI and blockchain from our last conference. Truly impressive, wasn't it?"

George nodded, his eyes meeting Radhika's. "Absolutely. Radhika, your perspectives were a highlight. I've been looking forward to hearing more from you too," he said, genuinely.

Radhika blushed slightly at the attention but maintained her composure. "Thank you, George. It's always a pleasure to discuss ideas with passionate individuals."

Mr Mehta excused himself to get a drink from the bar counter, leaving the trio alone. Sensing an opportunity, David leaned in closer to Radhika and began spouting cheesy, tech-themed one-liners.

"If you were a block in my blockchain, Radhika, I'd never let you get mined," David said with a playful smirk.

Radhika laughed, much to George's displeasure. He clenched his jaw, trying to maintain his composure.

"That's all David? Just one cheesy one-liner?" Radhika replied jokingly.

David, noticing George's reaction, continued, "Are you a neural network? Because my heart beats in sync with you."

Radhika giggled again, and George's frustration grew. "David, don't you think it's a bit much?" George interjected, his tone strained.

"Oh, come on, George! It's all in good fun. Besides, Radhika seems to appreciate a bit of tech romance," David retorted, his eyes gleaming with mischief.

Radhika, sensing the tension, decided to play along. "Actually, George, David's lines are quite charming. Maybe you should take notes," she said with a wink, adding fuel to the fire.

George bristled, his ego bruised. "I prefer genuine conversations over cheesy pick-up lines, Radhika," he said, his voice firm.

David laughed, enjoying the sparring. "Relax, George. Not everyone can appreciate the art of blending tech with romance."

Radhika, however, began to feel uncomfortable as David's lines became increasingly intrusive. He moved closer, invading her personal space. "You know, Radhika, we could make quite the pair. Imagine combining our talents—unstoppable," he said, his voice lowering seductively.

Radhika's smile faltered. She glanced at George, her eyes pleading for help and her eyes rolling upwords. George stepped forward. "David, I think your girlfriend Reshma just walked in and is coming this way," he said, his tone a bit shaky. David jumped up and spun around looking left and right. He looked taken aback but quickly recovered, flashing a confident smile. "Reshma. Aah! Old flame, not my girlfriend Radhika, just an acquaintance". Reshma walked straight up to them. "Busy! David?" she asked sarcastically, ignoring everyone around. "No, babe! George was introducing me to his girlfriend," David stuttered, raising his hands in mock surrender. He turned to Radhika, "Nice meeting you, Radhika." David and Reshma walked away. George sat down at a vacant chair near Radhika.

Radhika turned to George, her expression grateful. "Thank you, George. I appreciate that."

George smiled warmly, "Anytime, Rani. I couldn't just stand by and let him make you uncomfortable."

She smiled back, a genuine warmth in her eyes. "Jealous? Oh!? Well, you can be quite the hero too, you saved me (Ha! Ha!). "

CHAPTER THREE

Christmas in Goa

Ten days breezed by with nothing romantic happening. George tried his best to focus on events and the happenings around him, but he could only find himself thinking about Radhika. At one conference, he stood before a room of tech enthusiasts, his mind wandering. "That's why change has to be ... Radhika," he said, his voice trailing off.

The audience was silent for a moment before George quickly corrected himself, flushing slightly. "I meant radical. Change has to be radical."

Radhika, who was present, noticed and was a bit perturbed. She wasn't looking for a love connection right now, but she found this slip amusing. Despite herself, she found George charming and nice. She loved the attention too, as she hardly interacted with people, especially with young men around her age. His genuine interest and occasional awkwardness were endearing.

Christmas in Goa was something very special. Goa, with its rich Portuguese ancestry, has a very Mediterranean culture, celebrating Christian festivals with as much fervour as Indian festivals. The ten-day conference included three days of sightseeing and a boat cruise on the River Mandovi on Christmas Eve.

As the boat set sail on the tranquil waters of the Mandovi, the festive spirit was palpable. Fairy lights adorned the vessel, and the scent of freshly baked Christmas treats wafted through the air. George found himself next to Radhika on the deck, the soft glow of the lights reflecting in her eyes.

"It's beautiful, isn't it?" George said, his voice soft.

"Yes, it is," Radhika replied, her gaze fixed on the distant lights of Panjim shimmering on the water.

George hesitated before speaking again. "Radhika, I know we've only known each other for a short time, but I feel like... I don't know, like I've known you forever."

Radhika turned to him, a gentle smile on her lips. "I've enjoyed our conversations, George. You're different from anyone I've met before."

Encouraged by her response, George continued. "I think I'm starting to more than like you, Radhika. I know it's sudden, and I don't want to make you uncomfortable, but I needed to tell you."

Radhika's smile faded, and she took a deep breath.

"George, I appreciate your feelings. Truly. But I come from a very conservative background. A relationship is not even an option for me. And you being a Christian, would be an absolute disaster for my uptight caste-conscious family. Ha! Ha! They would probably be shocked."

George felt a pang of disappointment but nodded, understanding the weight of her words. "I understand, Radhika. I just wanted you to know how I feel. And regardless of what happens, I'm here for you."

Radhika reached out and squeezed his hand. "Thank you, George. That means a lot to me."

George and Radhika moved to the top deck of the vessel, away from the lively crowd below. The moon hung low in the sky, casting a silvery glow over the tranquil waters of the Mandovi. The cool breeze ruffled their hair as they stood side by side, gazing at the shimmering reflection of the moon on the river's surface.

"It's peaceful up here," George remarked softly, his eyes still fixed on the horizon.

"Yes, it is," Radhika agreed, her voice barely above a whisper. "It's a nice change from the hustle and bustle of the city."

George turned to her, his expression thoughtful. "I wanted to share something with you, Radhika. I lost my father when I was young. It was just my mother and me after that. She did her best to raise me, but I suppose I was a bit spoilt."

Radhika giggled "Only a bit spoilt? The way you spend money like water..." She then looked at him with empathy. "I'm sorry to hear about your dad, George. Losing a parent is never easy. How did your mother manage?"

"She worked hard, but we were financially well-off, thanks to my father's investments and my mother taking over my dad's business. I never really had to worry about money," George admitted. "But that also meant I never really learned the value of it. I have not learnt to save money for a rainy day, as it's always been sunshine at home."

Radhika nodded, her gaze returning to the moonlit water. "I understand. My family has always valued hard work. My mum has terminal cancer, and it's been a difficult journey for us. But we've always been there for each other.

We worked hard to reach where we are now, and I've learned to appreciate the value of money and the importance of being careful with money and people."

George's heart ached at her words. "I'm so sorry to hear about your mum, Radhika. It must be incredibly tough for you and your family."

"It is," she admitted, her voice tinged with sadness. "But we find strength in each other. We have a big family, and we've always supported one another through thick and thin."

George reached out and gently took her hand, giving it a reassuring squeeze. "You're amazing, Radhika. The way you handle everything with such grace and strength... it's inspiring."

Radhika smiled at him, a soft, grateful smile. "Thank you, George. It means a lot to hear that."

They stood in comfortable silence for a moment, simply enjoying the serenity of the night and the warmth of each other's presence. The soft sound of the water lapping against the boat and the distant hum of the festivities below created a cosy, intimate atmosphere.

"Do you ever think about the future?" George asked, breaking the silence.

"Sometimes," Radhika replied. "But it's hard to plan too far ahead when there's so much uncertainty. I try to focus on the present and make the most of every moment."

"That's a good way to live," George said thoughtfully. "I guess I've always been more focused on the here and now, not really thinking about what comes next."

Radhika looked at him, her eyes reflecting the moonlight. "Maybe it's time to start thinking about it, George. The future is important, and so is planning for it."

George nodded, a smile playing on his lips. "You're right. Maybe it's time for a change. And who knows? Maybe that change starts tonight."

Radhika's smile widened, and she leaned a little closer to him, the warmth of their connection growing stronger. "Maybe it does."

As they stood together under the moonlit sky, their conversation flowed easily, filled with shared dreams, hopes, and the beginning of a bond that neither of them had expected. The night was theirs, and in that moment, the world seemed just a little bit brighter.

CHAPTER FOUR

A Shocking Discovery!

A few years had passed since George and Radhika had first met at that fateful tech conference in Goa. Their relationship had grown deeper with each passing day, blossoming into a bond that was both unspoken and undeniable. They continued to meet as often as they could, usually accompanied by their mutual friends, David and Reshma. The four of them often reminisced about the early days, joking about their initial encounters and the moments that had brought them together.

On this particular evening, they found themselves in a quaint restaurant in Bandra. The place was charming, with its vintage décor, soft lighting, and a garden that was perfect for evening strolls. The atmosphere was warm and welcoming, and the friends settled into their favourite corner, where laughter flowed as easily as the wine.

David, who had undergone a significant transformation in his life, was still the same old jokester. He had reorganised his priorities and found a new sense of purpose, but his penchant for cheesy techie jokes remained intact.

"So, why did the computer go to the doctor?" David asked, grinning mischievously.

"Oh no, here we go again," Reshma groaned, but a smile tugged at her lips.

"Why?" George played along, leaning back in his chair.

"Because it had a virus!" David declared, laughing at his own joke.

Radhika and Reshma exchanged amused glances while George chuckled. Despite the predictability of David's humour, it always managed to lighten the mood.

As the conversation turned to more serious topics, they discussed their future plans. David spoke excitedly about his latest project, and Reshma shared her aspirations of starting her own business. George and Radhika listened, their hands brushing occasionally under the table, each touch sending a spark of electricity between them.

After dinner, David and Reshma decided to take a stroll in the restaurant garden. The two wandered off, leaving George and Radhika alone at the table. The soft glow of the candles on their table cast a warm light on Radhika's face, making her eyes sparkle.

Radhika suddenly reached across the table and took George's hand in hers. She looked at him, her gaze intense and filled with unspoken emotions. "George, I've been thinking a lot about us," she began, her voice soft.

George's heart raced as he looked into her eyes. He could see the depth of her feelings, the love that had grown between them over the years. "Rani, I feel the same way. I can't imagine my life without you," he confessed, squeezing her hand gently.

In a sudden flash, the sound of the restaurant door opening with a bang abruptly interrupted their moment. Radhika's father and brother strode in, their faces set in stern expressions as they spotted George and Radhika immediately and made a beeline towards their table.

George quickly dropped Radhika's hand and stood up, his heart pounding. "Hello, Mr. Mehta," he greeted, trying to keep his voice steady.

Mr. Mehta glared at him, his eyes cold. Radhika's brother, Rajat, stepped forward and pushed George back into his seat. "Sit," he commanded, his tone harsh.

George complied, his mind racing. Mr. Mehta nodded at Rajat, who then turned his attention to Radhika. "But, Papa," Radhika began to protest, her voice shaking.

"Come," Mr. Mehta growled, his eyes never leaving George's.

Radhika reluctantly stood up, her eyes filled with tears as she glanced back at George. As they left the restaurant, George could hear Mr. Mehta and Rajat yelling at her.

"A Christian, a loafer!" Mr. Mehta's voice was filled with anger.

"That's why I tell Papa not to take you to functions," Rajat added, his voice dripping with disdain. "I should have realised during our Goa trip, but I trusted you." Said Mr. Mehta disappointed.

"Have you seen how dark his skin tone is?" retorted Rajat as they exited.

George sat there, his heart breaking. He had known that their relationship would face obstacles, but hearing those harsh words directed at Radhika was almost unbearable. He watched helplessly as the love of his life was dragged away, the warm and happy evening shattered by the harsh reality of their situation.

Moments later, David and Reshma returned to the table, their faces lit up from their stroll. They immediately sensed the tension in the air.

"George, what happened?" Reshma asked, concern etched across her face as she sat down.

George took a deep breath, struggling to keep his emotions in check. "Radhika's father and brother just showed up. They saw us together and... it wasn't good. They took her away."

David frowned, his playful demeanour vanishing. "What did they say?"

George ran a hand through his hair, feeling the weight of the evening pressing down on him. "They were furious. Her brother pushed me back into my seat and told me to sit. Her father glared at me the entire time. They called me... a Christian loafer and said they didn't want her seeing me."

Reshma reached across the table, placing a comforting hand on George's arm. "I'm so sorry, George. That sounds awful."

George nodded, feeling a mix of anger and helplessness. "I knew it wouldn't be easy, but I didn't expect it to be this hard. I love her so much, and I can't stand the thought of losing her."

David leaned back in his chair, his brow furrowed. "This is a tough situation. Her family's very traditional, and they're not going to accept you easily. But you've got to decide if you're willing to fight for her."

"I am," George said firmly. "But I don't want to make her life harder. I don't want to put her in a position where she has to choose between me and her family."

Reshma squeezed his arm reassuringly. "Radhika is strong, George. She'll fight for what she wants too. But you need to be there for her, support her. This isn't just your battle; it's hers too."

David nodded in agreement. "We're here for you, mate. Whatever you need, we'll help you through this."

George felt a surge of gratitude for his friends. "Thank you. I just hope Radhika knows that I'll always be here for her, no matter what happens."

Reshma smiled softly. "She knows, George. She knows."

Back home, Radhika found her family gathered in the garden sit-out. The tension in the air was palpable, and she knew what was coming.

"I don't want to discuss this," Radhika said angrily, crossing her arms.

"Christian boy? Really?" her sister Rina chimed in, her tone incredulous. "Hmm, is he handsome?"

"Shut up, Rina," Radhika retorted, her patience wearing thin.

"Oh no, black, Goan-looking chap, like our driver Robert, haha," laughed Rajat, his words dripping with disdain.

"You're not going out anywhere anymore," her dad, Mr. Adil Bhai Hira Ram Mehta, said angrily.

Though she was 21, her family was very patriarchal, a mould she often wanted to break.

"Think about your mother's health," snapped her brother.

"Do you have a pic of him?" giggled her younger sister Rina, finding the situation humorous.

Radhika looked at her mum, seeking support.

Rani-Ma, her mother, looked at all of them and said in a soft yet commanding voice, "Leave us alone, everyone. I want to talk to Radhika alone."

"But Mum..." Rajat began, surprised.

"Now, please!" she said sternly.

"Someone's going to get it now," mumbled Rina as she left.

Rajat went off sulking, pounding his fist on the wall as he headed to his room.

"You too," Rani-Ma said to her husband Adil Bhai.

Her tone was firm, and he left. As soon as the others were out of earshot, she turned to Radhika and said loudly, "What's all this nonsense going on with you? Do you have no shame?"

The family smirked as they left, but Radhika was dumbfounded. She shared a special bond with her mother, and this reaction was unexpected. But then, Rani-Ma winked at her and pulled her into a hug.

"Sit down, beta," she said gently, guiding Radhika to a chair. "Tell me about George."

Radhika took a deep breath, feeling the warmth of her mother's embrace. "Mum, he makes me so happy. He's kind, intelligent, and he respects me. He respects our culture, our traditions."

Rani-Ma listened intently, her expression softening. "But his religion, Radhika... Are you going to convert to Christianity?"

"No, Mum," Radhika replied firmly. "He's very understanding. He respects all religions and cultures. He doesn't expect me to change who I am. We've talked about it, and he supports my beliefs."

Rani-Ma sighed, looking into her daughter's eyes. "Your happiness means everything to me, Radhika. But your father and brother... They won't understand. They'll think the worst."

"I know, Mum," Radhika said softly. "But I love him. And he loves me. Isn't that what matters?"

Rani-Ma hugged her again, tighter this time. "Love is important, beta. More than anything else. If he makes you happy and respects you, then that's what counts. But you'll have to be strong. This won't be easy."

Radhika nodded, tears brimming in her eyes. "Thank you, Mum. I needed to hear that."

"Just promise me one thing," Rani-Ma said, pulling back to look at her daughter. "Be true to yourself. Don't change for anyone, not even for love. If George truly loves you, he'll accept you as you are."

"I promise, Mum," Radhika said, a smile breaking through her tears.

Rani-Ma looked thoughtful for a moment, then spoke again, her voice gentle. "Tell me, how did you two meet?"

Radhika's face softened as she recalled the memory. "We met at a conference in Goa. It was a bit of a disaster at first. George was giving a speech, and he accidentally said my name instead of 'radical'. He was so embarrassed, but it was kind of sweet."

Rani-Ma chuckled. "That does sound endearing. What happened after that?"

"We started talking during the breaks, and I realised how genuine he is. He's passionate about his work, but he's also... he's got this warmth, Mum. He listens, really listens, and he cares about what I think."

Rani-Ma's eyes softened further. "And you think you're in love with him?"

Radhika hesitated, then nodded. "I think so. I'm still figuring it out, but every time we're together, I feel this... connection. And he's made it clear that he loves me, that he accepts me as I am. He's not asking me to change anything about myself."

"That's important," Rani-Ma said, squeezing her daughter's hand. "But you know your father and brother will be difficult."

"I know," Radhika sighed. "But I don't want to lose him. He makes me happy in a way I've never felt before."

Rani-Ma's expression grew serious. "Love is precious, Radhika. If you believe he's worth fighting for, then fight. But be wise. Take your time. Make sure this is what you truly want."

"I will, Mum," Radhika promised. "Thank you for understanding."

Rani-Ma smiled and kissed her forehead. "I just want you to be happy, my dear. And if George is the one who makes you happy, then I will support you."

They sat there for a while, holding each other, drawing strength from their bond. The garden around them was quiet, the tension of earlier replaced by a calm understanding.

CHAPTER FIVE

A Tricky Proposal!

The Mehta residence was alive with the bustle of activity. The living room, adorned with vibrant Gujarati decorations, exuded a festive air, yet there was an underlying tension that encompassed the evening. The aroma of freshly cooked delicacies like Rotla (a thick, unleavened flatbread made from millet flour), Dabeli (a savoury snack with potatoes, spices, and a variety of condiments and chutneys like green chutney, tamarind chutney, and mango chutney filled the house, mingling with the scent of flowers and incense, creating a sensory essence that was both inviting and formal.

Radhika sat in the corner of the room, her beauty a striking contrast to the dark sad mood she felt. Dressed in a rich blue sari with intricate gold embroidery, she looked every bit the epitome of grace. Yet, her heart was heavy, and her mind was preoccupied with thoughts of George. Her gaze wandered to the window, hoping for a distraction from the reality of her predicament.

Mr. Mehta had orchestrated the evening meticulously. Mukesh, the suitor from a respected family within their caste and community, had arrived with his parents. Mukesh, an NRI working for a prestigious multinational computer hardware firm in the USA, was a well-accomplished professional. He exuded confidence and charm, his tailored suit and polished shoes reflecting his international status. The families were engaged in exchanging gifts and pleasantries, their conversation a dance of formality and cautious enthusiasm.

Mukesh's mother, a graceful woman draped in a silk sari, offered her warmest regards, her eyes twinkling with maternal pride.

Mukesh's father, a distinguished man with a penchant for business acumen, had arrived with an array of impressive gifts that spoke volumes about their family's wealth and sophistication. He brought in a collection of exquisite Indian artefacts, each a masterpiece of craftsmanship. There were intricately carved wooden sculptures from Jaipur, delicate hand-painted miniature paintings from Rajasthan, and stunning brass statues of deities from Tamil Nadu.

The Mehta's had not shied away as well. To show their status, they had prepared for this very occasion for a whole month. In addition to their regular traditional items, there were high-end imported décor that showcased their global connections. A sleek Bang & Olufsen sound system gleamed from one corner. The dining room table was graced with a set of Waterford crystal glasses, each piece sparkling under the chandelier's light.

For Radhika, Mukesh's family had got her a Cartier watch with a mother-of-pearl dial and diamond accents, a symbol of timeless elegance. Mukesh's father had also brought along a selection of gourmet treats from Fortnum & Mason, London, including luxurious hampers filled with fine teas, biscuits, and preserves. As they were setting it all on the table, Mukesh also placed a limited-edition Montblanc pen set on the coffee table, opening its polished-wood box to display the fine craftsmanship.

The pièce de résistance was a Louis Vuitton trunk, a classic piece of luggage that epitomised luxury travel. Rina was already in love with this charming and handsome Suitor in her own childish way.

"He's so handsome and rich too, Radhu! Marry him and then take all his stuff and disappear with George", she said pretty confidently to Radhika.

Radhika was not in a mood for jokes or any form of humour. She brushed off the remarks, pretending that she didn't hear. The girl in her was excited on receiving such classy gifts, but somehow it still wasn't impressive enough to win her heart over. Her heart was already gifted with love to George and nothing in the world was going to change that.

As the families gathered, the atmosphere was a blend of tradition and modernity. The Mehta's were visibly impressed, the grandeur of the gifts adding to Mukesh's already favourable impression. Mr. Mehta's eyes lingered on the Cartier watch, while Rajat examined the Montblanc pens with a mix of admiration and envy.

The conversation flowed smoothly, Mukesh's father engaging everyone with his polished manners and insightful discussions on business trends and market opportunities. Despite the warmth and hospitality, an undercurrent of tension remained, particularly between Radhika and her father. The opulence of the gifts did little to ease her internal struggle, as her thoughts kept drifting to George and the promise she had made to him.

As the evening progressed, Mukesh's charm became apparent. He engaged in conversation with Rajat, discussing their shared interests in technology and business. Mukesh's insights into the latest advancements in computer hardware were met with genuine interest, and Rajat, ever eager to impress, responded with equal enthusiasm.

"You have a wonderful daughter," Mukesh's father said to Mr. Mehta, his voice filled with admiration. "We believe this match would be mutually beneficial for both our families."

Mr. Mehta nodded, a smile of satisfaction on his face. "Radhika is our pride and joy. We want the best for her, and we believe this union will surely be advantageous."

Mukesh, meanwhile, was focused on Radhika. His eyes followed her every move, though she remained distant, her heart clearly elsewhere. Despite his polished manners and the aura of sophistication, Radhika's thoughts were firmly fixed on George. To avoid her longing getting evident, she excused herself and walked to the kitchen. "Excuse me Geo... Err, sorry Mukesh ji, I need to check something in the kitchen." Before Mukesh could respond, Radhika gave him a half-smile and exited the living room.

In the kitchen, Radhika tried to steady her nerves as she poured herself a glass of water. The weight of the evening's expectations felt like a physical burden. Her phone was in silent-mode but she could feel it buzz frequently. She knew George was calling her, and each unanswered call added to her mounting anxiety and definitely to his as well.

Meanwhile, at home George was now beginning to panic, his heart heavy with worry. He had called Radhika several times, each call going unanswered. The uncertainty was unbearable, and he felt helpless as he imagined the possibility of losing her.

Their last conversation replayed in his mind, her words echoing with a mix of reassurance and urgency.

"I won't marry anyone else, George," she had said. "But you need to step up. Show my family that you are serious, that you love me enough to take care of me and respect our family culture. The fact that you're the wrong religion, caste, creed and even colour is itself a nightmare for my dad and brother. My mother understands and tells me to always follow my heart, but listen to my gut feeling…" Radhika is tired. She inhales deeply and sighs as she mumbles.

"This is a tricky proposal George"

George understood the gravity of her words. "Radhika…I feel we should…" There was a sudden click and Radhika had cut his call.

Darkness on a Full Moon Night!

George walked up to his mother, his heart heavy with a mix of sadness and frustration. "Why did she suddenly cut the call?" "What could have happened? " "Did her dad catch her on the phone with me" George was Why He had been trying to reach Radhika every few minutes, but each call went unanswered, the silence amplifying his fears. His mother, Martha, noticed the tension in her son's eyes and beckoned him over with a warm, knowing smile as she said

"Isn't the full moon simply beautiful tonight, George?"

George put his arms around her as he inhaled deeply. He knew that she knew that something was bothering George. Martha had always been George's greatest confidante, the one person he could turn to when life felt uncertain. She had a gift for understanding him in ways no one else could, and George cherished the bond they shared. As he sat down next to her, a powerful memory came to mind, one that had shaped his life in ways he hadn't fully realised until now.

In the memory, George was a young boy, perhaps ten or eleven, sitting on the front porch of their home, his face buried in his hands. He had just experienced the sting of disappointment after not being selected for the school football team. It felt like the end of the world to him, his dreams dashed in an instant.

Martha had joined him on the porch, carrying two steaming mugs of hot chocolate milk. She sat down beside him, her presence a soothing balm to his wounded pride. "What's the matter, George?" she asked gently, her voice filled with empathy.

"I didn't make the team, Mum," George had replied, his voice choked with emotion. "I tried my best, but it wasn't enough."

Martha had smiled, a wise and tender smile that seemed to hold the universe's secrets. "George, my son, sometimes our best efforts don't lead to immediate success. But every setback is just a stepping stone on the path to something greater. You must never let a temporary defeat define your future."

She had then told him a story about her own childhood, about how she had once dreamed of becoming a dancer but had been told she wasn't good enough. Instead of giving up, she found new avenues to express her passion through teaching and performing for small community gatherings.

"You have a fire in you, George," she had said, brushing his hair back affectionately. "That fire will guide you through the darkest nights and light your way to success. Remember, life is not about avoiding failure, but about learning from it and continuing to burn bright."

The memory faded, leaving George with a sense of warmth and clarity. Now, as he faced uncertainty with Radhika, he realised that Martha's words were as relevant as ever. He understood that he needed to trust in his love for Radhika, be patient, and find the courage to face whatever lay ahead.

Returning to the present, Martha placed a comforting hand on his shoulder. "George, whatever you're facing now, remember that you're not alone. Love has its trials, but it's worth fighting for. And no matter what happens, I'm here for you."

Her unwavering support filled him with a renewed sense of determination.

Her gentle yet firm advice had helped shape him into the man he was today. Whether he was facing a minor setback or a major life decision, her words always resonated with clarity and insight.

Their bond was strong, like a typical mother-son relationship. She understood him in ways that no one else could, often sensing his feelings before he even voiced them. Her encouragement had given him the courage to pursue his dreams, while her practicality kept him grounded.

Whenever it came to discussing his relationship with Radhika, George relied heavily on his mother's guidance. She was the one who had advised him to be patient, to give Radhika space to navigate her own complex emotions and family dynamics.

"Rani, please, just hold on." George's mind began imagining the worst possible scenarios. He couldn't shake the feeling that his entire world was on the brink of collapse.

He sat near his mother, helpless and anxious, his mind raced with a series of tormenting images. What if Mukesh was convincing Radhika to accept the proposal? What if her parents had already decided and were pressuring her into a decision she didn't want to make? Each unanswered call from Radhika sent his heart into a tighter spiral of defeat, of dread.

He imagined Mukesh, with his polished manners and undeniable charm, winning over Radhika's heart as they talked in the quiet corners of her home.

The whole week before today had passed in constant arguments with Radhika, like a hurricane destroying his world. No doubt Mukesh was handsome, smart, very rich, charming. George was feeling vulnerable and even though Radhika comforted him a thousand times and reassured him, there was only so much that she could do.George recalled the day before the proposal. They decided to meet at Rajesh Khanna Garden, a beautiful calming and peaceful garden nestled at New Gulab Nagar. George was waiting impatiently. George ducked suddenly behind a tree as she saw a Black SUV approach with authority and park in a corner. He recognised that vehicle. It was Rajat's. His heart began to race as the door opened and out stepped Ria from the passenger side. George began to think of excuses to give Rajat or the family. "What is Ria doing here with Rajat?" he thought aloud. Within a flash, Radhika walked around and Ria stood guard near the vehicle as she smiled and waved in George's direction.

"You nearly gave me a heart attack Rani," George excalimed breathlessly. Radhika giggled. They walked off and sat in a shaded quiet cozy corner near the garden oval under a tree. The late afternoon sun cast long shadows across the park, its golden light filtering through the trees as George and Radhika scanned the surroundings for familiar faces.

"Radhika, how can you expect me to be calm when Mukesh is right there, ready to take you away?" George said, his voice edged with desperation, still glancing nervously around to make sure they were alone.

Radhika sighed, keeping her voice low but firm. "George, I've told you countless times, I don't want to marry him. I love you."

"But your family, Radhika! They're pushing for this wedding, and Mukesh is... well, he's everything they want for you," George replied, his voice breaking slightly. "How can I compete with that?"

"It's not a competition, George. This isn't about Mukesh or my family; it's about us. We've talked about this. I'm not going to marry him," Radhika insisted, though her voice carried a note of weariness from repeating the same assurances.

George shook his head, frustration written across his face. "And yet every time I turn around, he's there. Your brother loves him, your parents are impressed by him, and—"

"And none of that matters to me!" Radhika interrupted, her eyes pleading with him to understand. "I've told you how I feel, and I've told my family too. But you have to trust me, George. You have to trust in us."

He paused, glancing around once more before looking at her with uncertainty. "It's hard, Radhika. I see how perfect he seems in their eyes, and it feels like I'm losing you before we've even had a chance to start."

She leaned closer, lowering her voice as she took his hands in hers. "You're not losing me. We've faced so much together already. We'll find a way through this too, but you have to believe that I'm standing by my decision."

George searched her eyes, seeing the truth in them but still feeling the weight of his fears. "I do believe you, Radhika. It's just... hard when everything seems stacked against us."

Radhika smiled softly, brushing a tear from his cheek. "I know it is. But remember, we've got each other. That's more than enough to face whatever comes our way."

He nodded slowly, her words sinking in. "What time are they coming tomorrow?."

"Geroge?," she said, her voice firm. "Now, let's not waste any more time discussing tomorrow. I have already decided in my heart.

"Decided what?" George asked, panic stricken all over his face.

"That it's going to be you, dumbo."

George sighed, pulling her into a tight embrace, still keeping one eye on the park path for any approaching figures.

"George! What are you thinking about so deeply?", It was Martha. George snapped back to his present moment. "About yesterday mom" He muttered. "She said not to worry and all, but Mukesh has been with them the whole day nearly and..." "And What?" his mother retorted. "Do you think she is so fickle to change her mind in a day?" George sighed deeply.

The thought gnawed at him, each passing minute feeling like an eternity. The fear of losing Radhika was a shadow over his thoughts, and the uncertainty was suffocating.

Back in a forgotten, lonely corner of the Mehta residence, Mukesh and Radhika were in a long conversation. Radhika told him about George, and Mukesh understood, though he was heartbroken as well. "I understand, Radhika," Mukesh said, his voice tinged with sadness but layered with sincerity. "When a man truly loves a woman, he wants her happiness more than his own. I've lost my love at first sight, but knowing you'll be with someone who adores you brings me some peace. I will think of what to say to your parents and mine too!" said Mukesh, dejected but comfortingly.

The sky now seemed brighter as the moon in full bloom seemed to be shining through, making Radhika feel much lighter and more relaxed. She was happy that Mukesh understood. Her burden and her head felt much lighter now. The night drew to an end with the stars twinkling and the city finally calming down to the silence of the night.

Back at home, George kept fidgeting with his phone, willing it to ring. Every passing second stretched into an hour as he waited for any sign that Radhika was still his, that she was safe, and that their love had not been lost in the chaos of expectations and traditions. Darkness enveloped him as his mother stroked his head and covered him with a sheet as he faded slowly to sleep.

This indeed was his darkest night.

CHAPTER SEVEN

Secret Meetings!

Over the week, after countless calls, heartfelt messages, and secret meetings, the air finally began to clear. George, who had been overwhelmed with anxiety and doubt, was slowly regaining his footing. He felt a wave of guilt for accusing Radhika of being unfaithful and was deeply sorry for demanding explanations that were never needed.

A week later, as George and Radhika sat on a secluded bench at their secret beach spot near Bandra, George took Radhika's hands in his. The small, hidden cove was their sanctuary, where the gentle waves lapped at the shore and the world felt miles away.

"I'm sorry," George said, his voice full of sincerity. "I let my fears get the best of me, and I hurt you with my accusations."

Radhika squeezed his hands gently, her eyes softening as she gazed at him. "I understand, George. It's been difficult for both of us, but I'm here with you. I always will be."

They sat in silence for a moment.

"I promise to be more patient and trust in what we have," George continued, his voice steady with newfound resolve. "I know now that we can face anything together."

Radhika smiled, her heart swelling with affection. "We're stronger than we think, George. We'll make it through this, one step at a time." Just as they began to relax soothingly in each other's company, a blaring SUV horn shattered the peace of the park. They looked up to see Rajat's car idling nearby.

"Damn!" Radhika and George muttered, almost simultaneously.

"Go home, George, I'll deal with him," Radhika said, her voice tinged with urgency.

"No," said George defiantly. "Let me talk to him as well."

Radhika shook her head, refusing to listen as she stormed towards Rajat. "So now you're following me?" she asked him aggressively, crossing her arms over her chest.

"Radhu, go sit in the car," Rajat replied, his face stern, leaving no room for argument.

Radhika hesitated for a moment, but something in her brother's tone made her reluctantly decide to obey. She turned back towards George with a worried glance before getting into the SUV.

As Rajat walked up to George, a thousand thoughts raced through George's mind. He tried to steady himself, bracing for the confrontation he knew was inevitable.

Rajat stopped in front of him, eyes narrowed. "Have you no shame, George? Sneaking around with my sister like some sort of criminal?" His voice was low, but the intensity was unmistakable. "You're disrespecting our family's wishes. Do you think that is some sort of joke? Ruining our self-respect."

George stood his ground, feeling the weight of Rajat's words but unwilling to back down. "I care about Radhika, Rajat. This isn't about disrespect. We love each other, and that's why we're here."

Rajat scoffed, making his hand into a tight fist, punching the air and then shaking his head. "Love? You think love justifies sneaking around behind everyone's backs? If you're really serious about her, and you have the guts, then do it the right way. Bring your mother and speak to my dad and the family. Taking her out like this, like a thief. This is your culture?"

George is burning with anger at these insults but stays calm. "I will, Rajat. I promise you, I'll do it the right way. But please, understand that we're not trying to hurt anyone and I absolutely respect her, you and your family too."

Rajat crossed his arms, considering George's words. "Until then, promise me you won't meet Radhika like this again, hiding in gardens or secret places here."

George took a deep breath, nodding solemnly. "I promise, Rajat. I'll not meet her hiding in gardens again."

"Good," Rajat said, finally letting some of the tension ease from his shoulders. "Make sure you keep that promise."

With one last look, Rajat turned and headed back to the SUV, signalling to Radhika to drive away as he followed them in his car.

CHAPTER EIGHT

No meetings in gardens!

One sunny afternoon, Radhika and her younger sister, Rina, were out shopping in the buzzing Bandra-Khar area, a shopping paradise in the ever-bustling city of Mumbai. They wandered into a colourful clothes shop, vibrant fabrics hanging from every corner. George, knowing their schedule, casually slipped in behind them, his heart racing with anticipation.

As Rina sifted through a rack of dresses, George approached with a grin. "Need any help choosing, Rina?"

Rina turned, her eyes widening in surprise before breaking into a smile. "George! What are you doing here?"

George chuckled, keeping an eye on Radhika, who was at the other end of the shop, her face lighting up at the sight of him. "Well, I have a knack for being in the right place at the right time."

Rina giggled, clearly enjoying the secrecy. "Didn't you promise my brother that you wouldn't meet Radhika?" she teased. From the corner of her eye, Radhika noticed George and began walking towards them. "I thought you promised Rajat that you wouldn't see me? So?" she said, feigning anger.

"Well, he actually said to promise that I wouldn't meet you hiding in gardens or secret places, and my exact words to him were, 'I promise that I'll not meet her hiding in gardens again,'" George reenacted his promise to Rajat.

"This is not a hiding place, and it's definitely not a garden," George replied with a twinkle in his eye. Radhika shook her head, happy to see him. Rina grabbed George's hand and said, "Come, help me pick out something nice, then." She dragged him off to Renuka's Store, where the latest women's dresses and western wear were always on display.

George walked in with Rina as Radhika followed from a distance. He picked up a dress. "How about this one?" he suggested, pulling out a vibrant blue dress that matched Rina's playful spirit.

Rina held it up against herself, twirling a bit. "Not bad, George. You might just have a future in fashion."

As George and Rina laughed over the vibrant blue dress, Radhika watched them with a growing sense of affection. She loved seeing George interact so effortlessly with her sister, their banter lightening the heavy burden of secrecy they carried.

George, noticing Radhika's gaze, smiled warmly at her. As they moved towards a quieter corner of the shop, he reached out, trying to hold her hand. Radhika playfully pulled away, her eyes sparkling with mischief.

"Not here, George," she whispered, glancing around to ensure no one was watching.

George chuckled, undeterred. "Why not? It's just a little hand-holding."

Before Radhika could respond, Rina popped up beside them, holding a dress against herself. "What do you think, Radhika? Does this colour suit me?"

Radhika sighed inwardly, her playful mood undeterred. "It looks lovely, Rina."

As Rina turned back to the rack, George leaned in closer to Radhika. "How about a quick kiss then?"

Radhika shook her head, giggling. "You never give up, do you?"

"Nope," George replied, a teasing glint in his eye. He leaned in once more, only to be interrupted by a passing sales clerk offering assistance.

Radhika stifled a laugh, watching George's expression of mild frustration. "You really should pick better moments," she teased.

As they finally made their way out of the shop, George tried once more, this time aiming for a quick peck on the cheek. Just as he was about to succeed, Rina appeared again, pulling Radhika towards another display.

"Come on, Radhika! You have to see this!"

George sighed dramatically, throwing his hands up in mock defeat. "I give up!"

Radhika burst out laughing, her heart swelling with affection. "Oh, poor George. Did you really want our first kiss to be like this? So unromantic."

George grinned, his frustration melting away. "You think this is funny, don't you?"

"Absolutely," Radhika replied, her eyes twinkling. "But don't worry. Good things come to those who have the patience to wait."

"'To those'? Who are the 'those,' Rani?" said George, slightly flustered.

Radhika laughed. "You! And no one else, don't panic," she said, shaking her head in mock disdain.

They continued shopping, the playful tension between them adding a delightful spark to the afternoon. Despite the constant interruptions, the connection between George and Radhika grew stronger. Each stolen glance and shared laugh deepened their bond.

A few weeks later, they managed another meeting, this time near Juhu Beach. It was late afternoon, and the sun was beginning to set, casting a golden glow over the waves. They found a secluded spot, hidden from prying eyes, where they could finally be alone.

Radhika looked out at the horizon, the wind gently tousling her hair. "I've missed you, George," she said softly, her eyes filled with longing.

George took her hand, pulling her close. "I've missed you too, Radhika. More than words can say."

They stood there for a moment, wrapped in each other's warmth, before George reached into his pocket and pulled out a folded piece of paper. "I wrote something for you," he said, his voice tender.

Radhika's eyes sparkled with curiosity. "A poem?"

George nodded, unfolding the paper and clearing his throat. He began to read, his voice filled with emotion:

"In the silence of the night,
Your name whispers through the stars,
A melody of love, pure and bright,
Guiding me, no matter how far.
Your eyes, the windows to your soul,
Reflect the dreams we dare to chase,
In your presence, I feel whole,
Lost in the magic of your embrace.
Though shadows may try to keep us apart,
Our love will forever shine,

For you are the keeper of my heart,
And I, eternally yours, divine. "

Radhika felt tears prick at the corners of her eyes, moved by his heartfelt words. "It's beautiful, George. Thank you."

George leaned in, brushing a strand of hair from her face. "It's how I feel, Radhika. Every word."

As the sun dipped below the horizon, casting a warm glow around them, George cupped Radhika's face in his hands and kissed her gently. She was first taken aback and then grabbed him and kissed him back with all her love. It was their first kiss, a moment filled with unspoken promises and a love that defied the odds.

The world around them faded, leaving just the two of them, lost in each other. For that brief moment, they forgot about the challenges they faced, focusing only on the love that had brought them together.

When they finally pulled apart, Radhika rested her head against George's chest, listening to the steady beat of his heart. "I love you, George," she whispered, her voice filled with certainty.

"I love you too, Radhika," George replied, holding her tight.

"*We'll find a way. No matter what, we'll be together.* "

"Have you decided how your going to meet us?" "Be Calm when you enter" "Don't dress to jazzily" "You know my mum likes you and though you've met her when we were shopping a few times, don't get all pally pally and arouse suspicion" Radhika was nervous. George grabbed her and kissed her hard.

"Best way to keep you calm" he said after he let go.

"George...." Radhika retorted breathlessly.

"Don't worry, Rani. I got this. Sunday is fixed"

• 45 •

This isn't easy!

The dawn of that fateful day broke clear and bright, casting a golden hue over the city. George and his mother, Martha, arrived at the Mehta residence, their hearts heavy with anticipation. George, clad in a finely tailored suit that masterfully blended traditional and modern styles, exuded a quiet confidence. Beside him, Martha radiated grace in a simple yet elegant sari, her warm smile a beacon of calm amidst the storm brewing within them both.

As they reached the door, George could feel his pulse quicken, the weight of the moment pressing down on him. With a steadying breath, he rang the bell. The door swung open to reveal Mr. Mehta, his expression a mixture of surprise and guarded curiosity.

"George, are you sure you want to waste your time and ours too?" Mr. Mehta's voice held a sharp edge, a hint of impatience threading through his words.

George felt his heart skip a beat but pushed forward, determination lighting his eyes. "Mr. Mehta, this is my mother," he introduced, gesturing towards Martha. She stood beside him, her gaze steady and kind.

Martha stepped forward, her voice soft yet firm, carrying with it the weight of years gone by. "Adil Bhai, it's been a long time," she began, her tone laced with the warmth of familiarity. "I remember how respected my late husband was, and I recall the times when he extended a helping hand to your family during those difficult days." Her words, though gentle, held the power of past kindness, a subtle reminder of the bonds that once existed between their families. "I hope we can find common ground here, for the sake of our children."

Mr. Mehta's eyes narrowed slightly, his gaze shifting between George and Martha. The room seemed to hold its breath as silence settled over them, the weight of unspoken words pressing down. The challenge in Mr. Mehta's eyes was clear, but beneath it, a flicker of uncertainty could be seen, perhaps a glimmer of the man he once was—a man who had known the value of friendship and loyalty.

Mr. Mehta's expression softened slightly at the mention of the past, though he maintained his stern demeanour. "Yes, I remember. Your husband was a good man," he acknowledged, albeit reluctantly.

Finally, Mr. Mehta sighed, a reluctant nod of acknowledgment following. "Let's sit down," he said, his voice losing some of its earlier harshness. As they moved into the living room, George couldn't help but notice the cautious glances exchanged among the Mehta family members, each of them weighing the implications of this unexpected meeting.

George looked around and then inhaled deeply to calm his nerves, determined to make his case. "Mr. Mehta, I love Radhika with all my heart. I understand the challenges we face, but I'm willing to work through them because she's worth it. I promise to respect your family and traditions."

Martha nodded in agreement, adding, "We're here because we want to build bridges, not tear them down. I know it's not easy, but love often finds a way through the hardest of barriers."

Mr. Mehta remained silent for a moment, his eyes flickering with a mix of emotions.

As they spoke, Rani-Ma appeared from the hallway. She moved Mr. Mehta aside with a playful yet firm nudge. "Namaste!" She said with a quick wink at George and a smile. "So this is the boy and his mother?" She asked Adil Bhai, pretending she had no clue to who George was. "Christian family?" She said deliberately.

Mr. Mehta, taken aback by his wife's unexpected interruption, muttered "Ya! This is the Boy George and his mother Martha Ji, Capt. Albert Ferns wife"

"Albert? Who gave us our first contract when we had a small business in Goa"

"Yeah!" Said Adil Bhai, hesitantly.

"Small world." Replied Rani-Ma.

Rani-Ma turned to George and his mother, her face softening into a welcoming smile.

As the tension in the room built, a slight creak at the door announced the arrival of the maid. She walked in carrying a tray laden with an assortment of traditional Gujarati snacks—dhokla, fafda, and khandvi. The unmistakable scent of mustard seeds and curry leaves filled the room.

George, who wasn't exactly fond of Gujarati cuisine, plastered on a smile and took a piece of dhokla. He chewed slowly, trying his best to hide his discomfort.

Rina, ever the mischief-maker, noticed his hesitation and grinned. "Come on, George, don't be shy. You should really try the khandvi—it's the best!" Without waiting for a response, she leaned over and piled more onto his plate, her eyes twinkling with mischief.

George shot her a mock glare from the corner of his eye, but he couldn't refuse. He nodded and took a bite, his face a mix of forced delight and silent endurance.

Rina stifled a laugh, clearly enjoying his predicament. "See? Isn't it just delicious?" she teased, as George continued to eat with exaggerated enthusiasm, each bite slower than the last.

George silently made a note to get back at her for this, but for now, he simply gave her a playful glare, finishing the last bite with a resigned sigh.

Rani Ma spoke "Let's hear them out, Adil Bhai. After all, this is about Radhika's happiness."

George nodded, appreciating Rani-Ma's support.

Mr. Mehta's eyes reflected a mixture of surprise and scrutiny. The living room was still abuzz with activity as the families exchanged pleasantries. Radhika's heart skipped a beat at the sight of George, and she watched with hope and anxiety.

Rani-Ma, always the voice of reason, stepped forward with a calm, authoritative presence. "George, we appreciate your honesty and your bravery. But this is a matter of great importance, and we must consider our family's traditions and values."

George's mother, standing beside him, added her support. "We have come here with a sincere request. My son loves Radhika deeply and is willing to embrace and respect your traditions while sharing his own. We ask for your blessing and the opportunity to prove our intentions."

The room fell silent as the family absorbed George's heartfelt plea. Mr. Mehta's gaze shifted between George and his daughter, whose eyes were filled with both hope and apprehension. Rajat, who had been silently observing, finally spoke up.

"This is not an easy decision," Rajat said, his tone guarded. "Our family values and traditions are important to us."

Radhika stepped forward, her voice trembling but resolute. "Papa, I love George. He respects me and my family, and I believe we can find a way to honour both our traditions and our love."

Mr. Mehta sighed deeply, the weight of the decision evident on his face. "We need time to discuss this among ourselves. This is not a decision we can make hastily."

George and his mother nodded in understanding. "Thank you for considering our request," George said earnestly. "We will wait for your decision with respect and hope."

As George and his mother were leaving, George turned back to look at Radhika and Mr. Mehta. He hesitated for a moment before speaking. "Sir, the State Conference for software is at the end of next week. I know you'll be there. May I have your permission to sit with you at the table and let Radhika be with me for the evening?"

Mr. Mehta appeared a bit taken aback by the request, unsure of how to respond. But before he could say anything, Rajat intervened with a slight grin. "I'll be there with my fiancée as well," he said. "We'll bring Radhika and drop her home. You can be together at the conference, but don't go disappearing to any gardens or hidden spots."

"Of course not, Rajat," George replied, relieved. "I will respect my promise and your wishes."

With a nod of approval from Mr. Mehta, George and his mum, Martha, left the Mehta residence. Radhika stood at the door dumbstruck by George's guts. She watched them leave, her heart filled with admiration for George's courage and respectfulness.

Once outside, Martha looked at her son with a proud smile. "Impressive, son! That was gutsy, asking her out like that, and it was respectful as well."

George chuckled, feeling a mix of relief and anxiety. "And damn scary, Mum, really damn scary."

Martha laughed softly.

The next evening, the Mehta household gathered once more, the remnants of the previous night's formalities replaced with a serious atmosphere. Mukesh and his family had left as nothing had materialised but they said they would wait for any change of heart or a decision. Martha and George did manage to create a decent impression. The weight of this decision at hand was intense.

As they were sitting around in the living room discussing Radhika's options, She suddenly looked up firmly, her eyes filled with a mix of frustration and determination. "Papa, Mama, Rajat, I understand what Mukesh represented. He's everything you wanted for me. But my heart belongs to George. He loves me for who I am, and I love him just as much."

Mr. Mehta's face grew stern. "Radhika, love is important, but so are stability and tradition. George may love you, but he comes from a different background. His lifestyle and our community's expectations might clash."

Rani-Ma looked deeply into Radhika's eyes. "We've seen you with George. Your happiness with him is undeniable. But are you ready for the challenges that come with such a relationship? The societal pressure, the family expectations?"

"Seen? When?" Said Adil Bhai reactively.

"I mean when they came over to our place, we saw them" Said Rani-Ma recovering swiftly from her slip-up.

Rajat, now slightly more serious, added, "And what about George's financial stability? He's a good man, no doubt, but he has no savings. Mukesh, on the other hand, is financially secure and can provide a comfortable life for you."

Radhika, her voice trembling with emotion, responded, "George might not have savings, but he has a big heart. He is creative, talented and earns enough to keep his lifestyle and mother happy. He respects me, my culture, and my family. He's willing to do whatever it takes to be with me"

Mr. Mehta's expression was still defiant. "Radhika, we want what's best for you. All this love and all is nonsense. It's your decision but sorry, we need a few months to really decide and think all this over. I'm not even sure about that Conference now. We will simply be encouraging them."

Rani-Ma placed a reassuring hand on Radhika's shoulder. "You know my health is getting worse. I may not have a few months. "Everyone reacted to her saying that.

Adil said "Please dear. Don't talk like that." He went up to her and held her hand as he looked in her eyes. Radhika hugged her mother in a tight embrace.

Rajat sighed with genuine concern. "Radhika, we just want you to be happy. If George is the one who makes you happy, we need to find a way to make this work."

Radhika, her eyes brimming with tears, nodded. "Thank you, Rajat. Thank you, Mama. Papa. I know this isn't easy, but I believe in George, and I believe in our love."

CHAPTER TEN

Surviving Love!

The day was finally set - Monday, October 19, 2015—a date that would forever be etched in the memories of George, Radhika, and their families. The wedding was to be a grand affair, blending the rich traditions of both their cultures. The day was meticulously planned, ensuring that both a Christian wedding and Hindu rituals would be celebrated with equal grandeur.

The church wedding was held in a historic cathedral, its Gothic architecture providing a stunning backdrop for the solemn ceremony. The soft strains of a pipe organ filled the air as Radhika, adorned in a resplendent white gown, walked down the aisle. Her face was veiled, but the sparkle in her eyes was unmistakable. George stood at the altar, his heart racing with love and anticipation. His tailored suit, sharp and elegant, was a blend of contemporary style with traditional touches, a reflection of the union taking place.

Rina and Rajat were the only members of the Mehta family present for the Christian wedding. They watched with quiet admiration as George and Radhika exchanged vows, their words resonating through the hallowed halls of the cathedral. It was a ceremony marked by reverence, each moment heavy with meaning.

The temple wedding, held in true Gujarati style, was an explosion of colour and culture. The mandap, intricately decorated with marigolds and jasmine, was the centrepiece of the ceremony. Radhika, now dressed in a vibrant red saree, looked every bit the traditional bride. Her hands were adorned with intricate mehendi designs, and her jewellery sparkled as brightly as the sacred fire that burned in the centre of the mandap.

Adil Bhai, along with Rina and Rajat, attended this ceremony, their presence lending weight to the occasion. The chanting of mantras filled the air, as priests performed the rituals that would unite the couple in the eyes of God and their families. The atmosphere was charged with spirituality and tradition, a stark contrast to the solemnity of the earlier church ceremony.

The reception that followed was held at the Grand Hyatt in Mumbai, an opulent affair that spared no expense. The ballroom was transformed into a wonderland of lights and flowers, with guests from all walks of life coming together to celebrate the union. The finest delicacies were served, and the air was filled with laughter, music, and the clinking of glasses.

The reception at the Mumbai Grand Hyatt was a breath-taking fusion of cultures, with the grandeur of the occasion reflecting the depth of George and Radhika's love. David and his girlfriend, among the few close friends invited, were engrossed in the festivities, their faces lighting up with every joyful moment.

As they approached the newlyweds, David grinned. "Well, George, you clean up pretty well. Didn't think you had it in you to pull off such a grand wedding!"

George laughed, glancing at Radhika with pride. "It wasn't just me, you know. Radhika made sure everything was perfect."

Radhika smiled, her eyes twinkling. "I had a lot of help from everyone, including George. We wanted a blend of both our worlds, and I think we managed it quite well."

David's girlfriend chimed in, "The mix of traditions is beautiful. The temple rituals were so serene, and the church wedding was simply divine."

Rina, standing nearby, couldn't resist a playful jab. "David, you're just lucky we let you in. I wasn't sure if you'd behave in such a sophisticated setting."

David shot her a mock-offended look. "Rina, you wound me! I can be sophisticated... when I have to be."

Rina chuckled, "I'll believe it when I see it."

David, not missing a beat, quipped back, "Well, I'm here, aren't I? And I haven't done anything too embarrassing - yet."

Yet, amidst the celebrations, there was a shadow of absence. Rani-Ma, Radhika's beloved mother, could not attend the wedding due to her ailing health. Her absence was felt keenly by Radhika, but the joy of the day was not diminished. Rani-Ma had blessed the union in her own way, her heart filled with happiness for her granddaughter.

The brightness of those wedding days was overshadowed two years later by a sudden and heart-wrenching turn of events. Rani-Ma, the pillar of the Mehta family, took seriously ill. Her cancer had entered its final stages. The family, usually so composed, found themselves in a state of panic. But it was George who stepped up, his calm demeanour and command over the situation providing a much-needed anchor.

As they rushed Rani-Ma to the hospital, the emergency team swiftly wheeled her into the ICU. The air was thick with urgency as doctors huddled together, their faces set with grave determination.

"Her condition is critical," one of the senior doctors murmured, scanning the monitors. "The tumour's growth has accelerated, and she's crashing. We need to stabilise her heart rate before we lose her."

"Prep for an emergency intervention," another doctor ordered, his voice cutting through the tension. "If we can manage her vitals, there's a chance she might regain consciousness, but the prognosis is dire."

As the medical team worked with precision, their movements a blur of coordinated chaos, George stood by, his hand gripping Radhika's. She was pale, her pregnant form trembling with fear, but George's steady presence was her anchor in the storm.

"The tumour's compromising her respiratory system," a nurse reported, glancing at the readings. "We're losing her."

"Get the crash cart ready," the lead doctor barked, his voice filled with urgency. The room buzzed with activity as the team fought against time, their every action a desperate attempt to pull Rani-Ma back from the brink.

Minutes felt like hours as they worked, the tension so thick it was nearly suffocating. George's fluency in English and understanding of the necessary formalities proved invaluable, as he navigated the paperwork and hospital protocols with a clear mind, allowing the family to focus solely on Rani-Ma.

Finally, after what felt like an eternity, the erratic beeping of the heart monitor began to stabilise. The doctors exchanged weary glances, their shoulders sagging with a mix of relief and resignation.

"She's stable, but only just," the lead doctor said, wiping the sweat from his brow. "She might regain consciousness, but... she doesn't have much time."

True to his words, Rani-Ma slowly opened her eyes, the room falling silent as her frail form stirred. Her breath was shallow, each inhale a monumental effort, but there was clarity in her gaze as she looked around at her family.

In the dimly lit room, the family gathered around Rani-Ma's bed, their hearts heavy with concern. Radhika, pregnant and emotional, held onto George's hand as they navigated the labyrinth of hospital corridors and the finality of the moment.

Rani-Ma, her voice weak but filled with love, reached out to Radhika and George, her frail hands holding theirs tightly.

"You have survived Love," she whispered, her eyes filled with a wisdom that only time could bring.

"Survive Life as well."

Her words hung in the air, a poignant reminder of the journey they had begun together. As they held her hands, tears streamed down their faces, knowing that her blessing was more than just words—it was a charge, a challenge, a final gift.

The long, steady beep of the heart monitor broke the hearts of everyone around. Tears flowed freely as they faced the reality they had feared most.

And with that, the most important chapter of their lives closed, leaving the door ajar for what was to come.

Surviving Life!

Book 2 will delve deeply into the journey of Radhika and George as they strive to survive life together.

Marriage, far from being a bed of roses, presents challenges that test even the strongest bonds. As their once unbreakable connection begins to fray, a single misstep—like a drop of black ink in a clear pond—casts a shadow over their lives.

Friends who once stood by them may turn away, leaving Radhika and George to navigate the turbulent waters of their relationship, struggling to find a way to endure and survive in the face of adversity.

> *"Surviving Life, the next volume in this trilogy, explores the strength required to endure the most intimate ups and downs that can threaten a relationship. It reveals how external interferences and the toxic influences of those who worm their way into personal spaces can spread their destructive poison, further testing the resilience of love."*

... TO BE CONTINUED